The Mouse
Was Out
at Recess

The Mouse
Was Out
at Recess

by David L. Harrison

illustrated by Eugenie Fernandes

Wordsong
Boyds Mills Press

To Norma and Victor Watts,
who always take time for others

—D. L. H.

Text copyright © 2003 by David L. Harrison
Illustrations copyright © 2003 by Eugenie Fernandes

Published by Wordsong
Boyds Mills Press, Inc.
A Highlights Company
815 Church Street
Honesdale, Pennsylvania 18431
Printed in China

Harrison, David Lee.
The mouse was out at recess / by David L. Harrison ;
illustrated by Eugenie Fernandes. —1st ed.
[32] p. : col. ill. ; cm.
Note: Sequel to Somebody Catch My Homework.
ISBN 1-56397-550-5
1. Homework — Poetry — Juvenile literature. 2. Children's poetry,
American. [1. Schools — Poetry. 2. American
poetry. 3. Humorous poetry.] I. Fernandes, Eugenie. II. Title.
811/ .54 21   PS3558.A6657M68 2003
2002108958

First edition, 2003
Book designed by LDLDesigns
The text of this book is set in 18-point Journal Text.
The illustrations are done in gouache, pencil, and
pen and ink.

Visit our Web site at www.boydsmillspress.com

10 9 8 7 6 5 4 3 2 1

Contents

The Bus 6

Today We Wrote Letters 7

My Essay on Birds 8

Donny's Picture 9

The Dog in School 10

The Mouse Was Out at Recess 11

Sidney 12

Bradley 14

Jessica 15

Listen to Me! 16

Mystery Lunch 17

Be Fair! 18

They Call It Science 19

Raise Your Hand If You Know the Answer 20

In the Hall 21

It's Better If You Don't Know 22

A Matter of Opinion 23

Homerun King 24

The Secret 25

Have It Your Own Way 26

Grade Card 27

Our Field Trip 28

Teacher's Eyes 30

We'll Be Back! 31

THE BUS

You know what's cool
About going to school?
Riding on the bus!

You wave at your friends
When the day just begins
And you're riding on the bus.

Some kids are new
But you wave at them, too
When you're riding on the bus.

Lazyheads snore
But the rest of us roar
When we're riding on the bus.

Old Man Jones
Just sputters and groans
When he's driving our bus.

"Stop that noise
Or I'll toss a few boys
Right off this bus!"

We don't know
If he'd really ever throw
Anybody off the bus.

So we try to settle down
When we see him frown
'Cause it is his bus.

And what's really cool
About going to school
Is riding on the bus!

TODAY WE WROTE LETTERS

Benji wrote the president.
Jenny wrote the mayor.
Matthew wrote the Pope himself
And even wrote a prayer.

Jonathan wrote an astronaut
Who just got back from space.
Me? I wrote to Santa Claus.
(You know—just in case.)

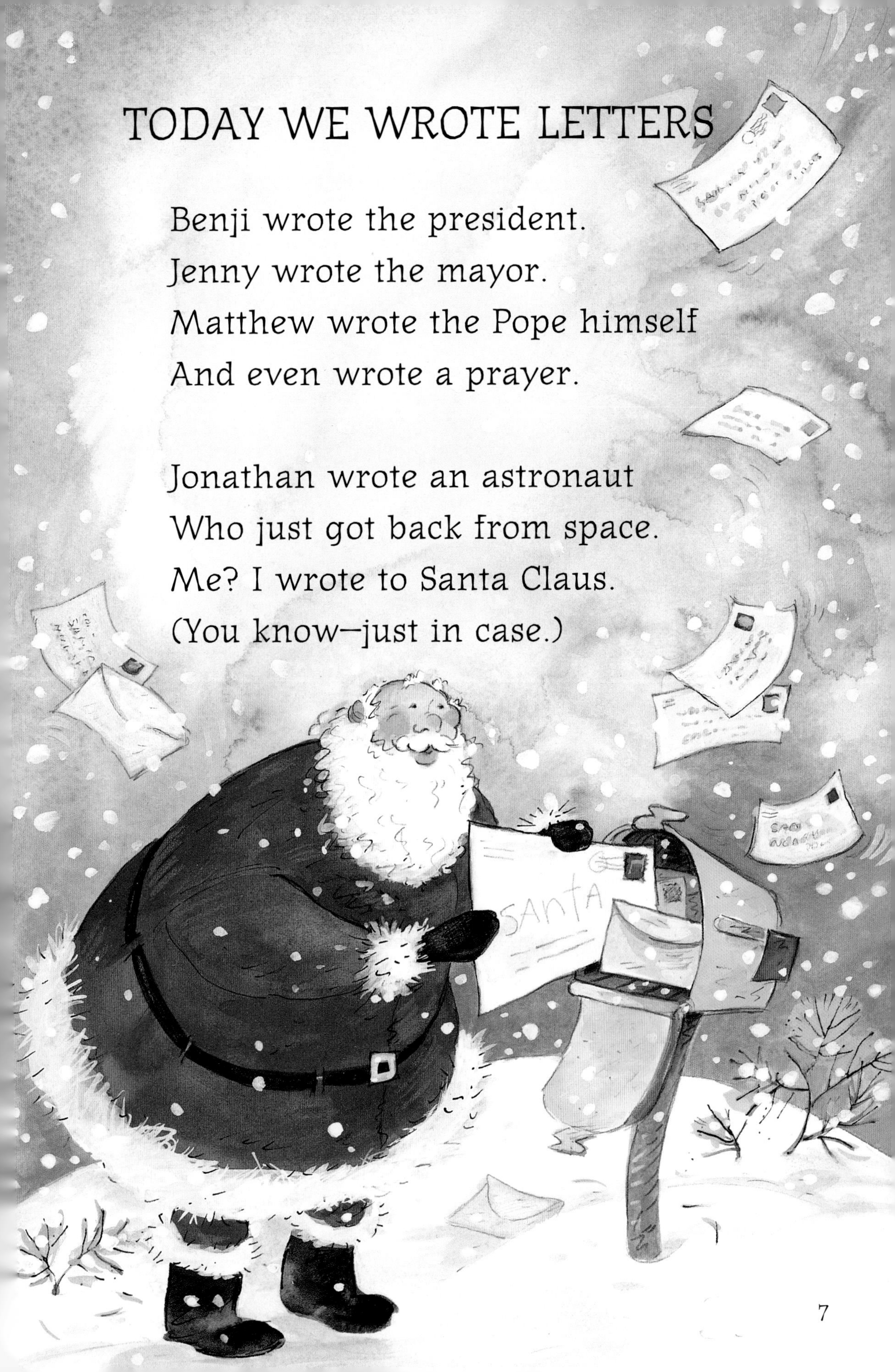
SANTA

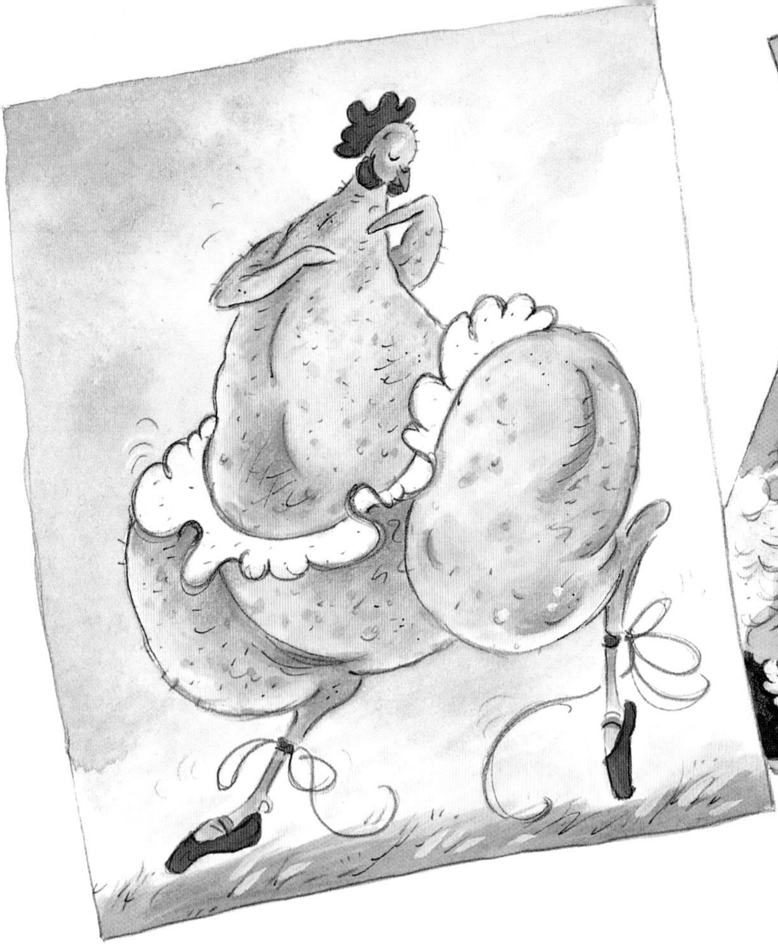

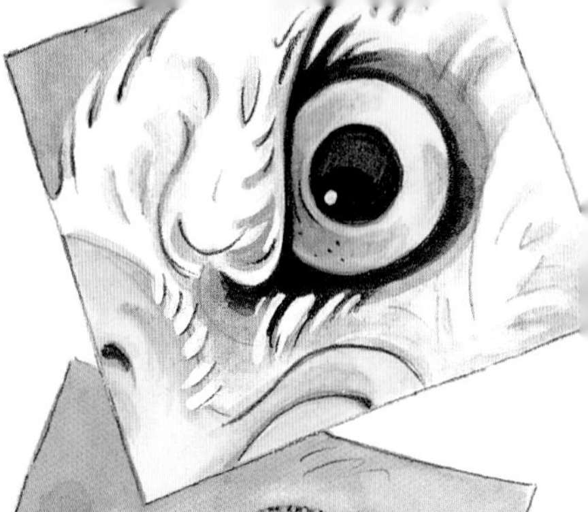

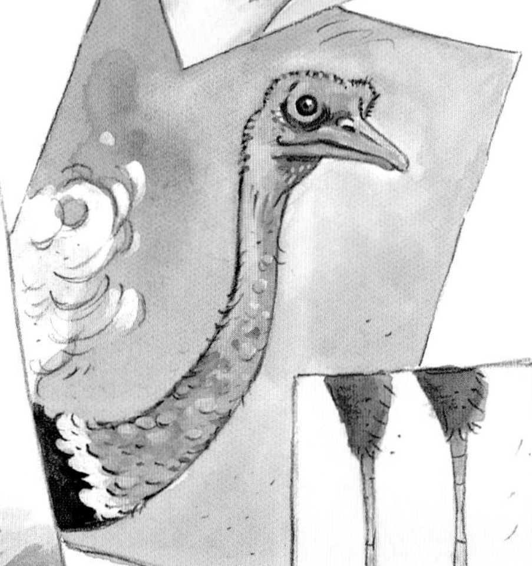

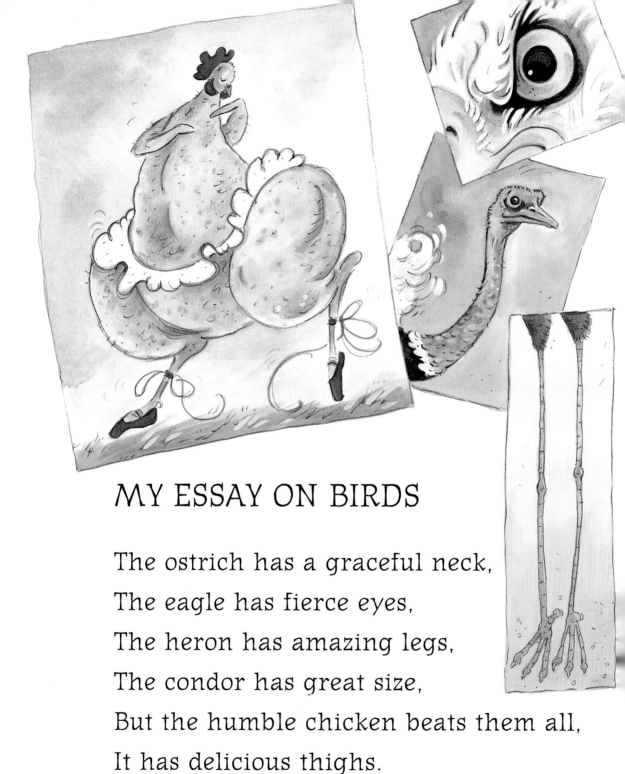

MY ESSAY ON BIRDS

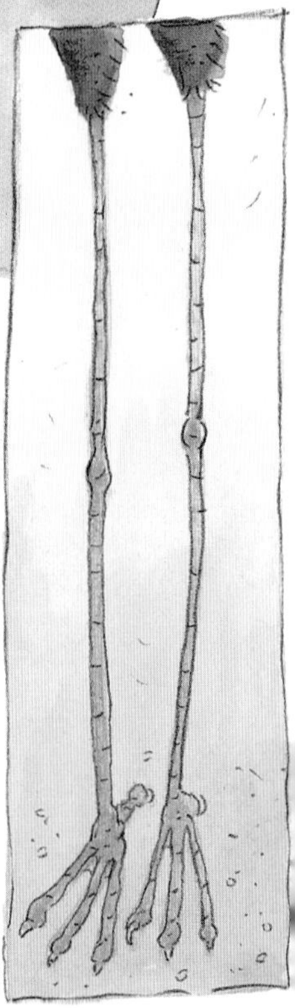

The ostrich has a graceful neck,
The eagle has fierce eyes,
The heron has amazing legs,
The condor has great size,
But the humble chicken beats them all,
It has delicious thighs.

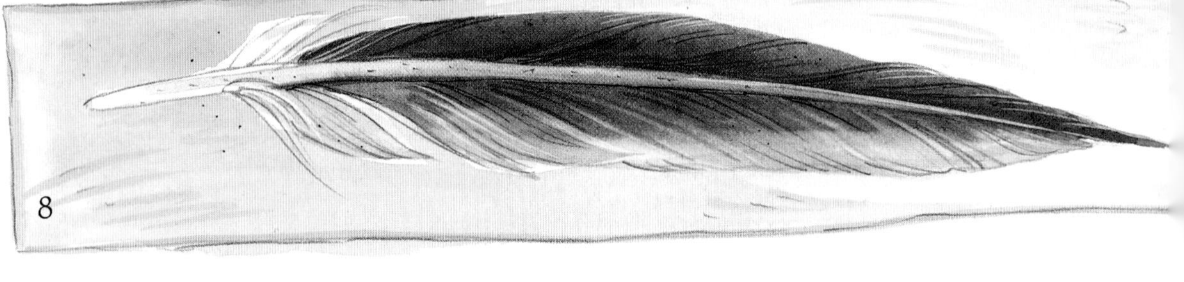

DONNY'S PICTURE

When Donny got an A in art,
He really was surprised!
When Teacher asked him what it was,
You should have seen his eyes!

We know something Teacher doesn't—
Donny's doggie did it.
He wagged his tail in Donny's paint!
Poor Donny can't admit it.

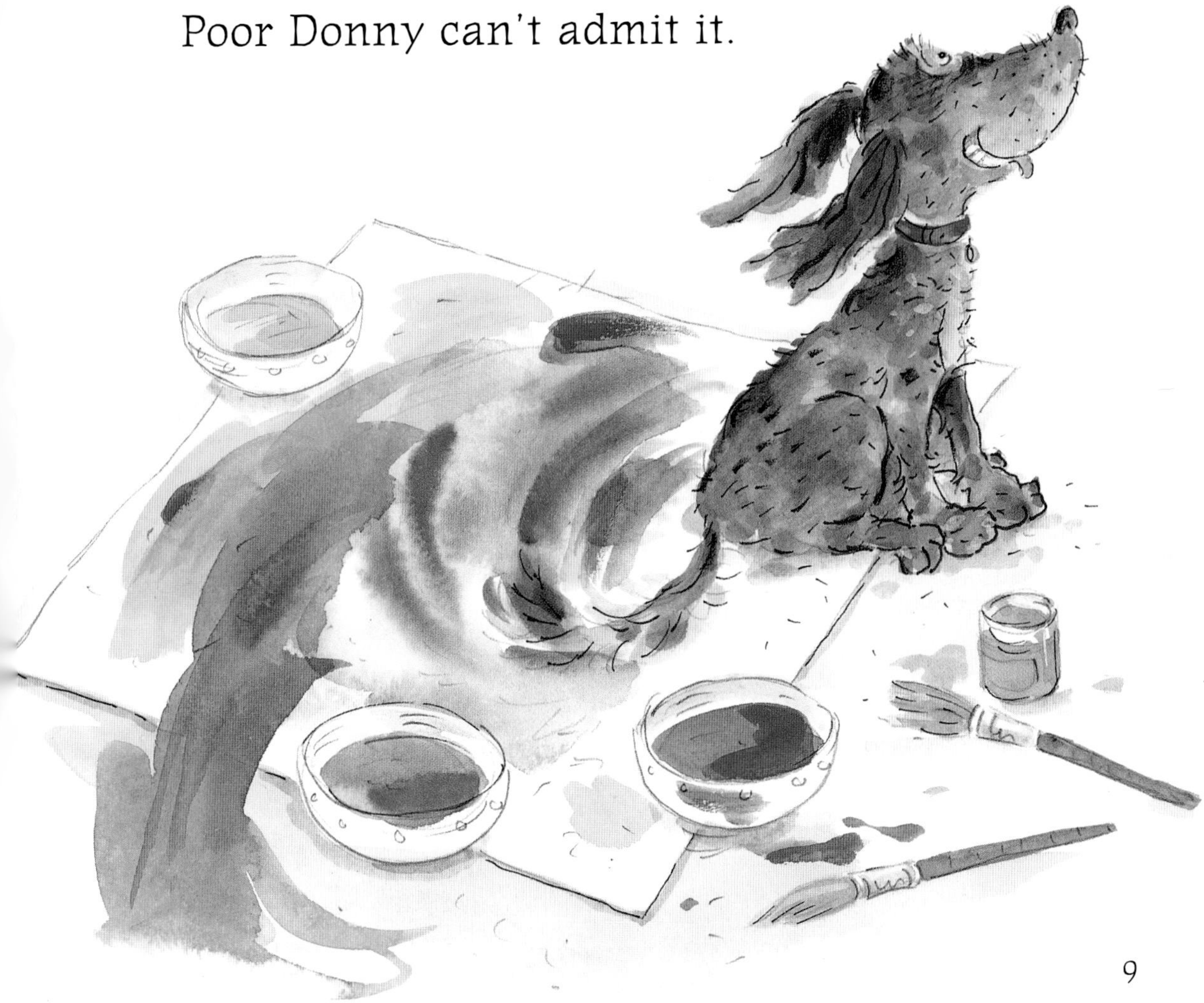

THE DOG IN SCHOOL

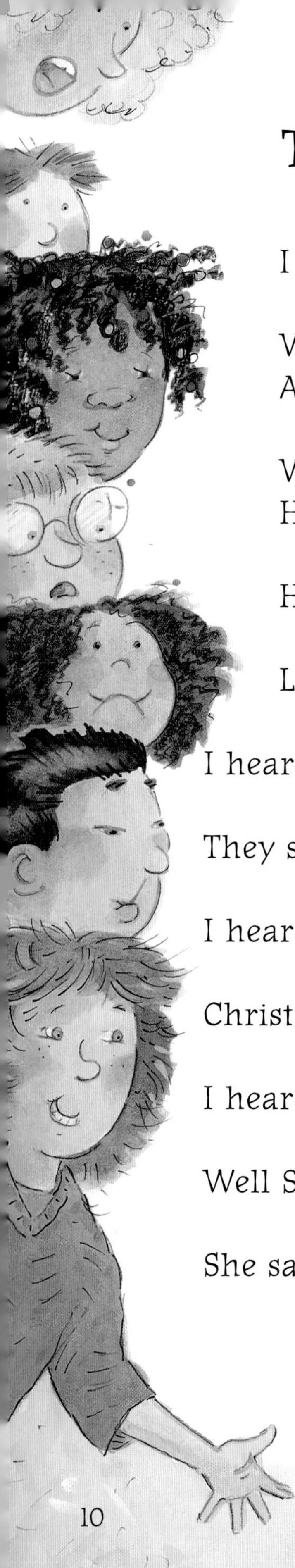

I heard he's big as a grizzly bear!

Well Cecie stopped me in the hall
And she said Ivan said he's small!

Well you know what I heard from Claire?
He's fatter than a butterball!

He's skin and bones I heard from Pete.

Latisha said he wouldn't eat.

I heard he stole a roll from Paul!

They say he's brown with reddish feet.

I heard he's mean and mostly white!

Christina said he wouldn't bite.

I heard he bit off Sasha's seat!

Well Sasha said that's simply drool.

She says there is no dog in school!

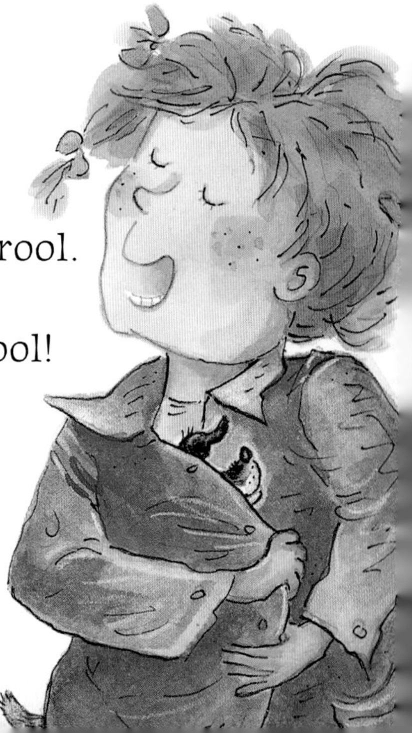

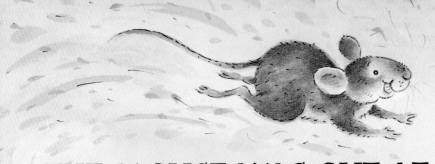

THE MOUSE WAS OUT AT RECESS

The mouse was out in class today
And out again at lunch.
No one knows who did it yet
But we have a little hunch.

The mouse was out at recess
And again this afternoon.
No one saw who let it out
But I bet we find out soon.

"Don't look at me!" says Bobby Gene,
His smile is sweet and sappy
'Cause every time the mouse is out
He looks just downright happy.

SIDNEY

"Lookit! Lookit!" Sidney said
And blew a bubble big as his head
In the hall
In front of Clifford Ball.

So what do you think old Clifford did?
Popped that gum all over Sid.
Sticky stuff blew everywhere
From Sidney's cuffs to Sidney's hair.
The ickiest thing I've seen in years
Was gummy wads in Sidney's ears.

Clifford laughed so hard he slid
Across the hall and into Sid.
"Help me!" Clifford cried. "I'm stuck!"
"Gross!" we yelled. "Extremely yuck!"

Stuck together like a ball
They rolled and tumbled down the hall
And every time they bumped a kid
The kid got glued to Cliff and Sid.

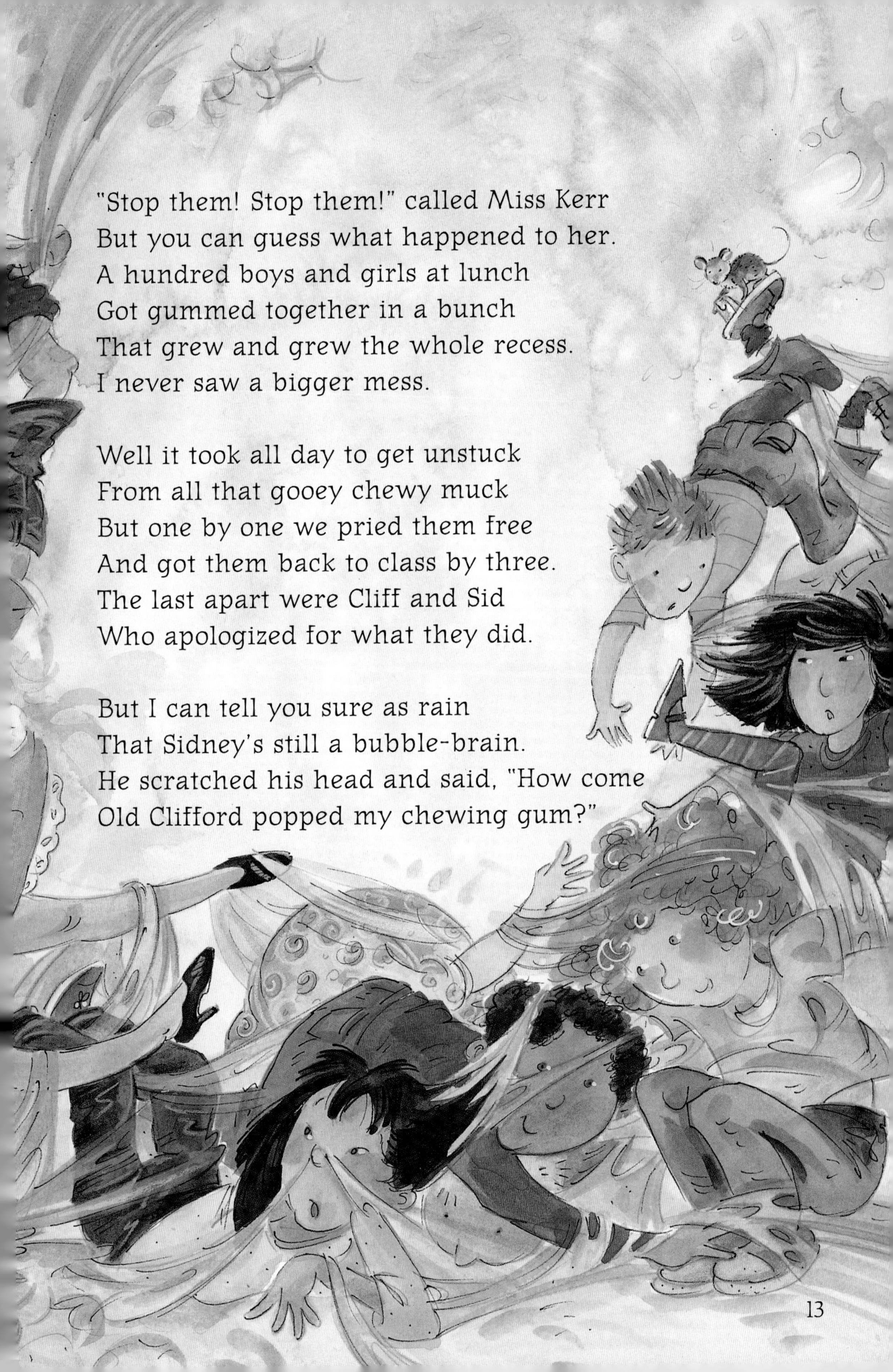

"Stop them! Stop them!" called Miss Kerr
But you can guess what happened to her.
A hundred boys and girls at lunch
Got gummed together in a bunch
That grew and grew the whole recess.
I never saw a bigger mess.

Well it took all day to get unstuck
From all that gooey chewy muck
But one by one we pried them free
And got them back to class by three.
The last apart were Cliff and Sid
Who apologized for what they did.

But I can tell you sure as rain
That Sidney's still a bubble-brain.
He scratched his head and said, "How come
Old Clifford popped my chewing gum?"

BRADLEY

Even when we study madly
No one ever matches Bradley.
We would be like Bradley gladly
But sadly he's the only Bradley.

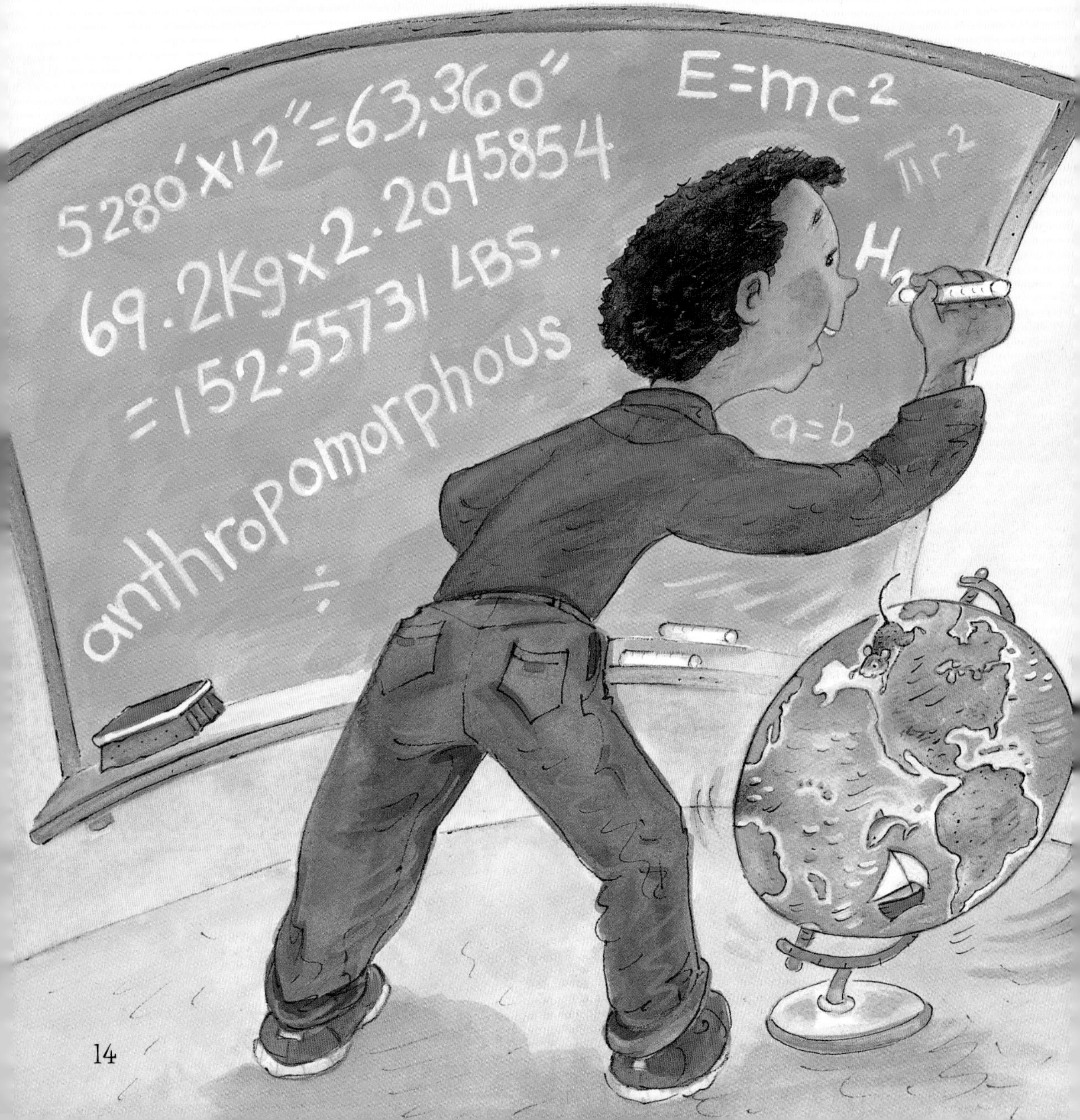
5280′x12″=63,360″
E=mc2
69.2Kgx2.2045854
=152.55731 LBS.
πr2
H2
a=b
anthropomorphous
÷

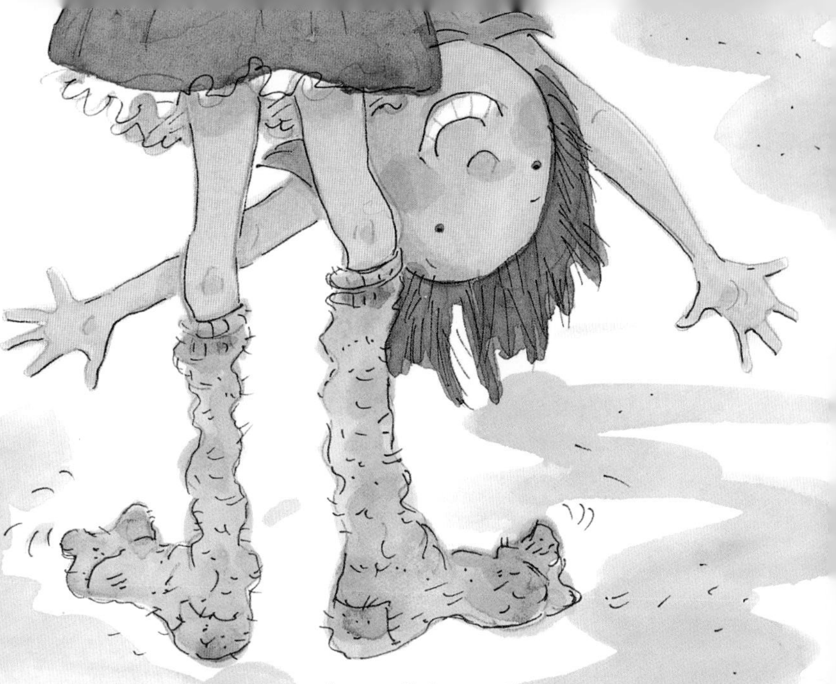

JESSICA

When Jessica wiggles her stinky old socks,
We stuff up our noses with cotton!
We gasp and we sigh,
We gag and we cry,
"Your socks are incredibly rotten!"

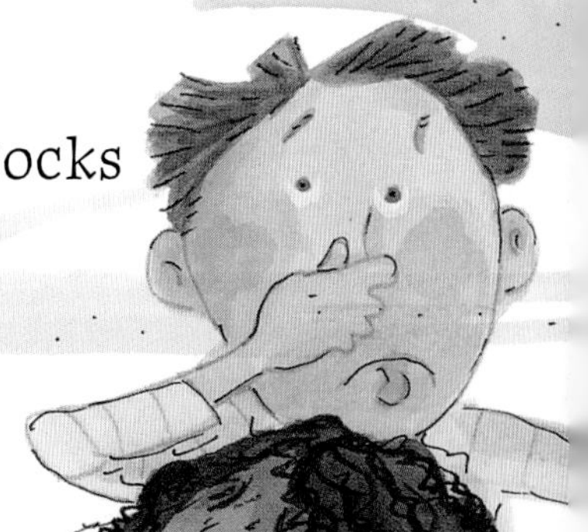

But Jessica wiggles those stinky old socks
All fuzzy with sweaty toe jelly
And she giggles with pride,
"When it's warm inside,
My socks are deliciously smelly!"

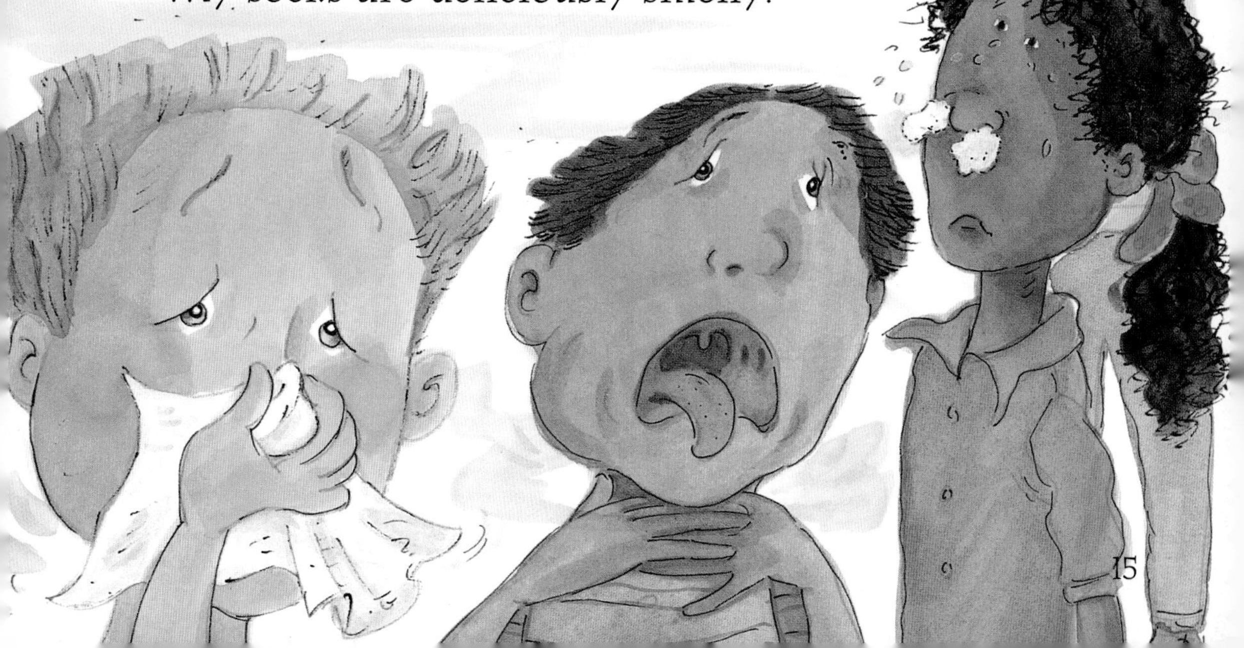

LISTEN TO ME!
Poem for Two Voices

(Boys)
Stay away from girls!
That's my advice to you!

And keep away

Are through!

I have an older brother
Who was a happy kid like you,
But once he started liking girls,
They turned his brain to goo!

So never talk to girls!

Boo!

As your very best friend,

It will ruin your life if you do!

(Girls)
Stay away from boys!

Stay away

Or your carefree days

I have an older sister
Who was a happy kid like you,
But once she started liking boys,
They turned her brain to goo!

So never talk to boys!
Don't let one even say

I'm warning you

It will ruin your life if you do!

MYSTERY LUNCH

Brother fixed my lunch today.
I've no idea what's in it,
But if he fixes it again,
Next time I hope he'll skin it.

I showed the thing to Mike who sniffed,
"What do you think it is?"
"Don't know," I said, "you want to trade?"
So Michael gave me his.

I took a look in Michael's sack
But there wasn't much to see
So I yelled at Jan and threw her his
And she threw hers to me.

"What do you have to eat?" I asked.
Janet rolled her eyes.
"Sister fixed my lunch," she said,
"Nothing I recognize."

It smelled so bad I couldn't look
So I traded back with Mike.
Skinned or not, my brother knows
The sort of stuff I like.

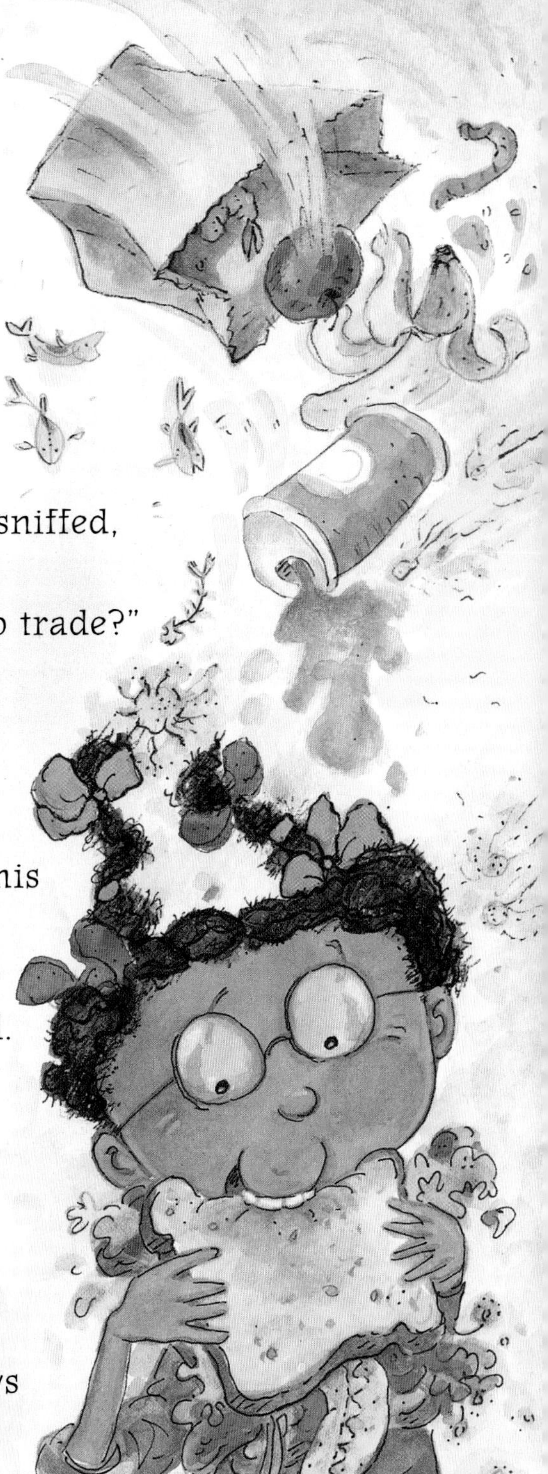

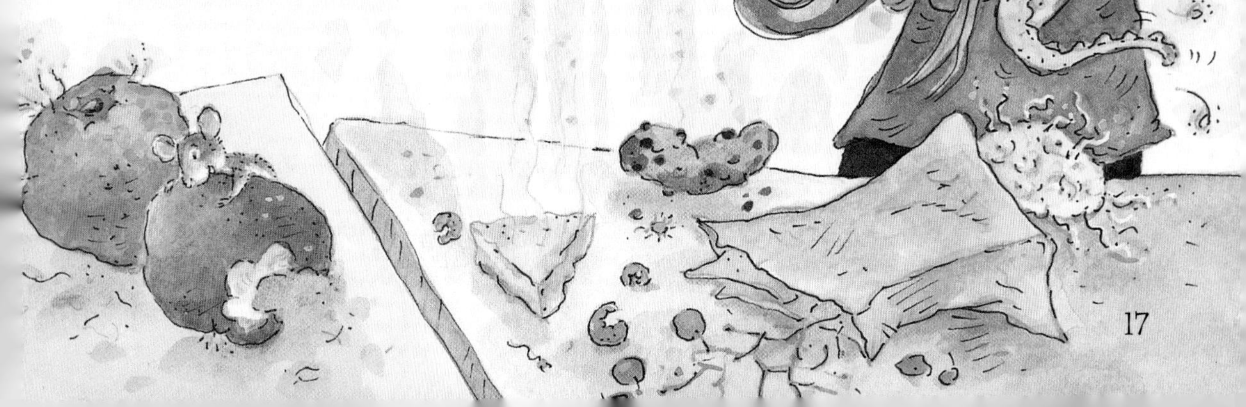

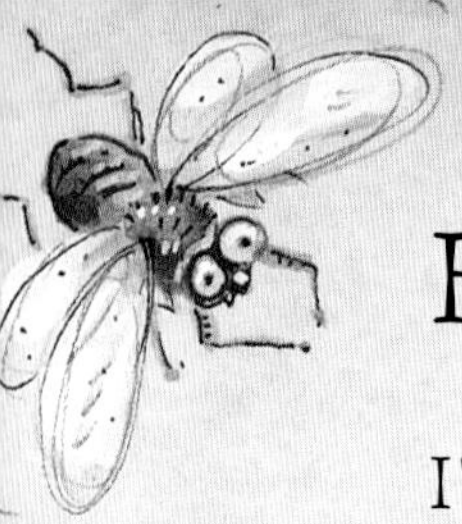

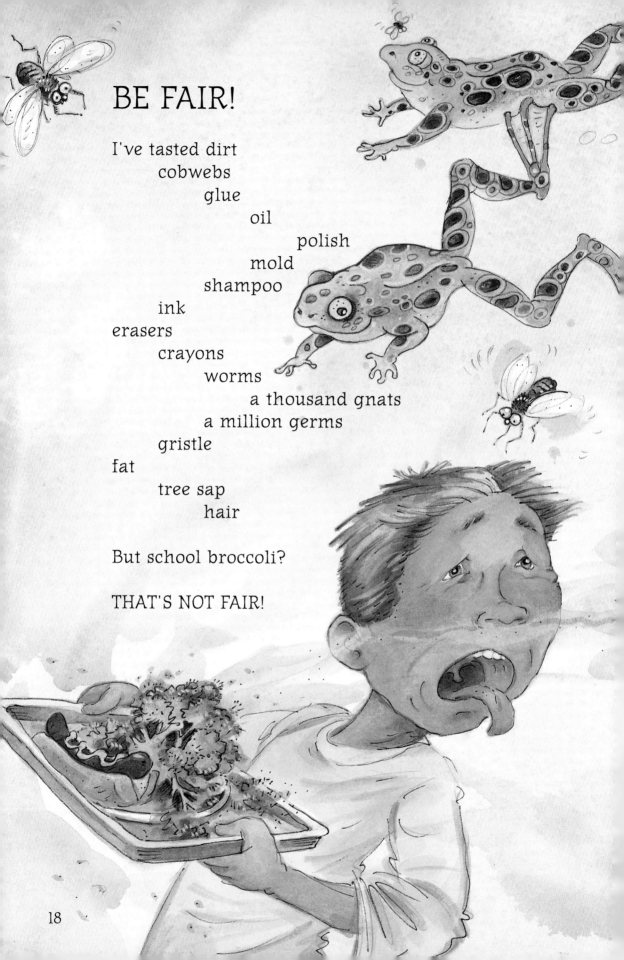

BE FAIR!

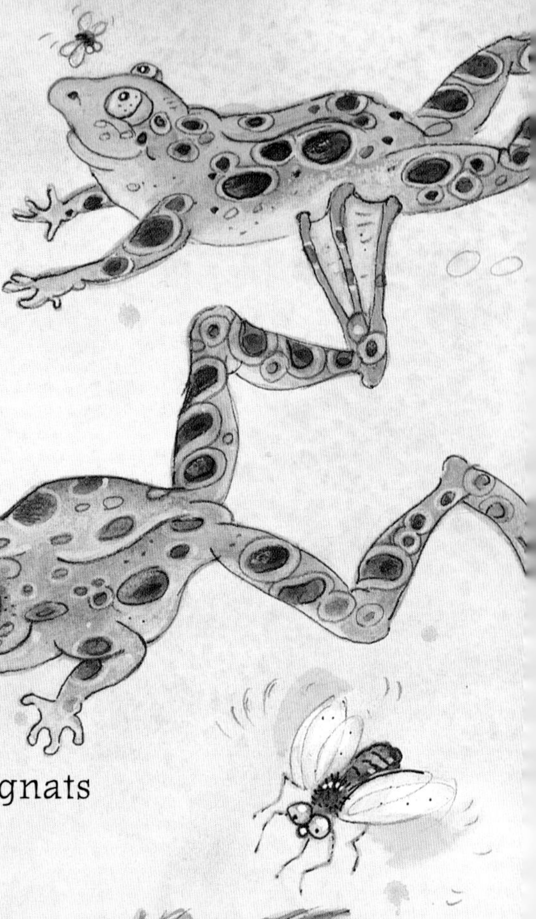

I've tasted dirt
cobwebs
glue
oil
polish
mold
shampoo
ink
erasers
crayons
worms
a thousand gnats
a million germs
gristle
fat
tree sap
hair

But school broccoli?

THAT'S NOT FAIR!

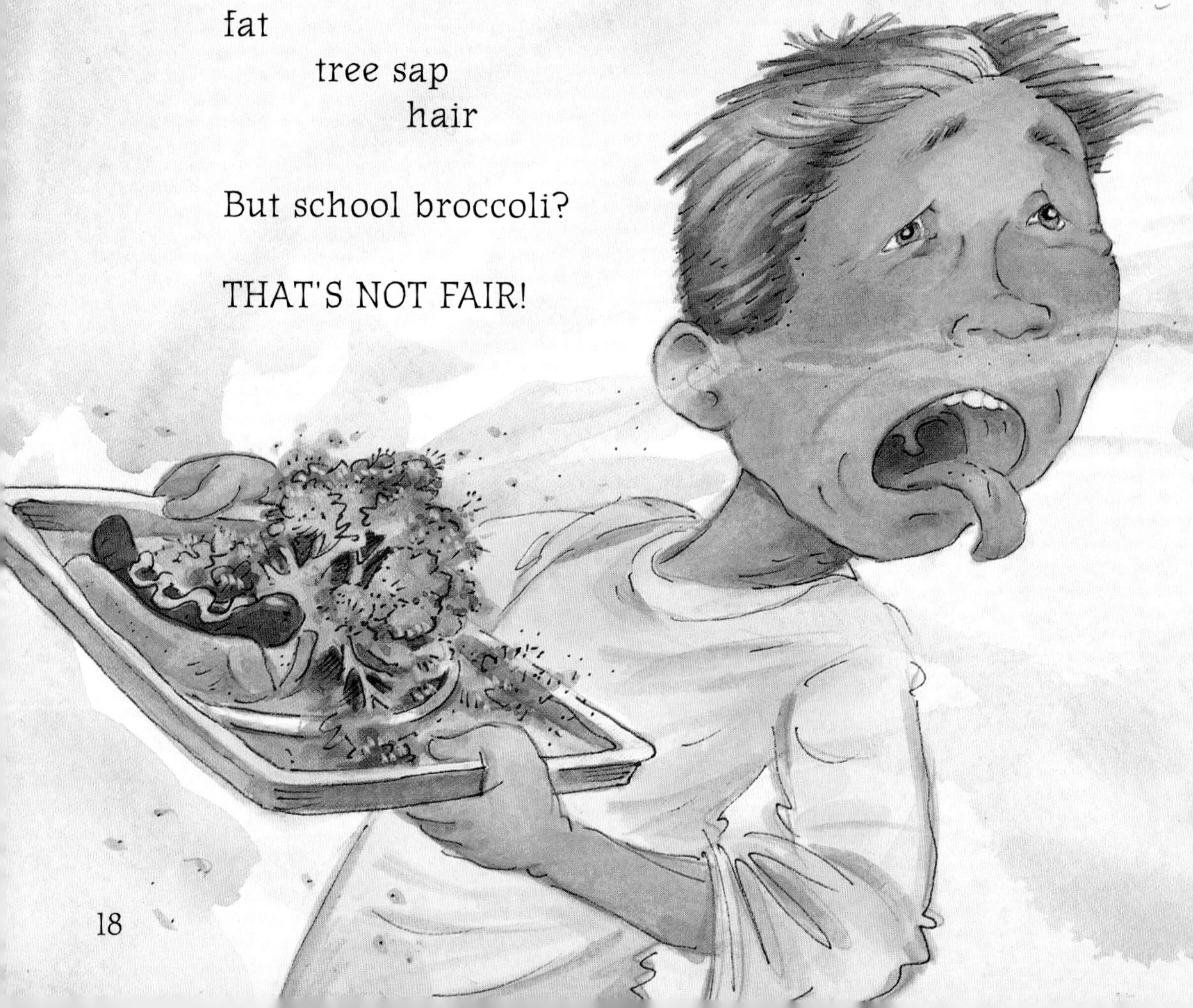

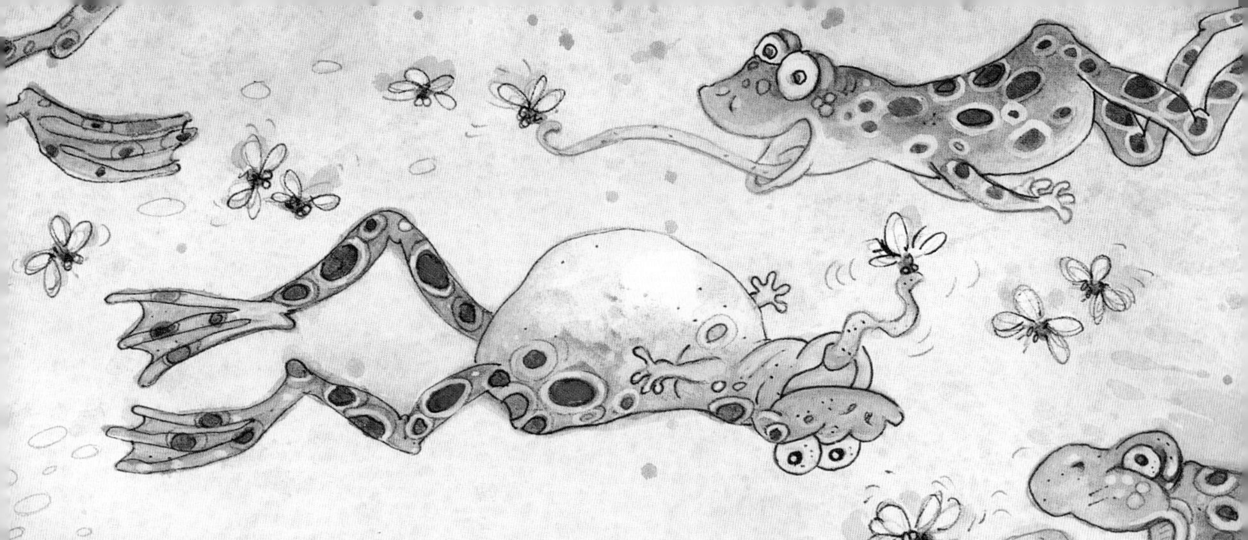

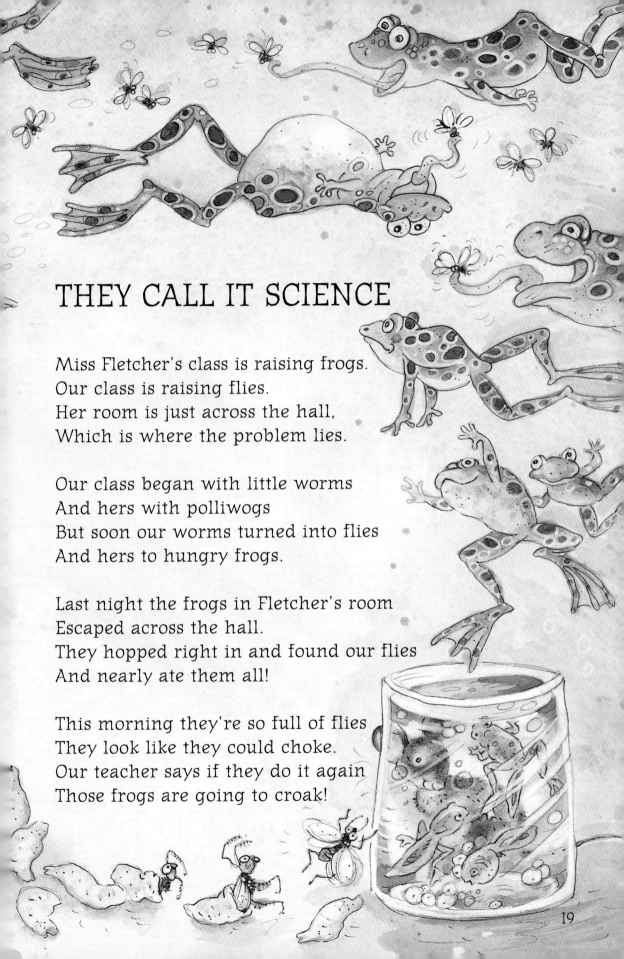

THEY CALL IT SCIENCE

Miss Fletcher's class is raising frogs.
Our class is raising flies.
Her room is just across the hall,
Which is where the problem lies.

Our class began with little worms
And hers with polliwogs
But soon our worms turned into flies
And hers to hungry frogs.

Last night the frogs in Fletcher's room
Escaped across the hall.
They hopped right in and found our flies
And nearly ate them all!

This morning they're so full of flies
They look like they could choke.
Our teacher says if they do it again
Those frogs are going to croak!

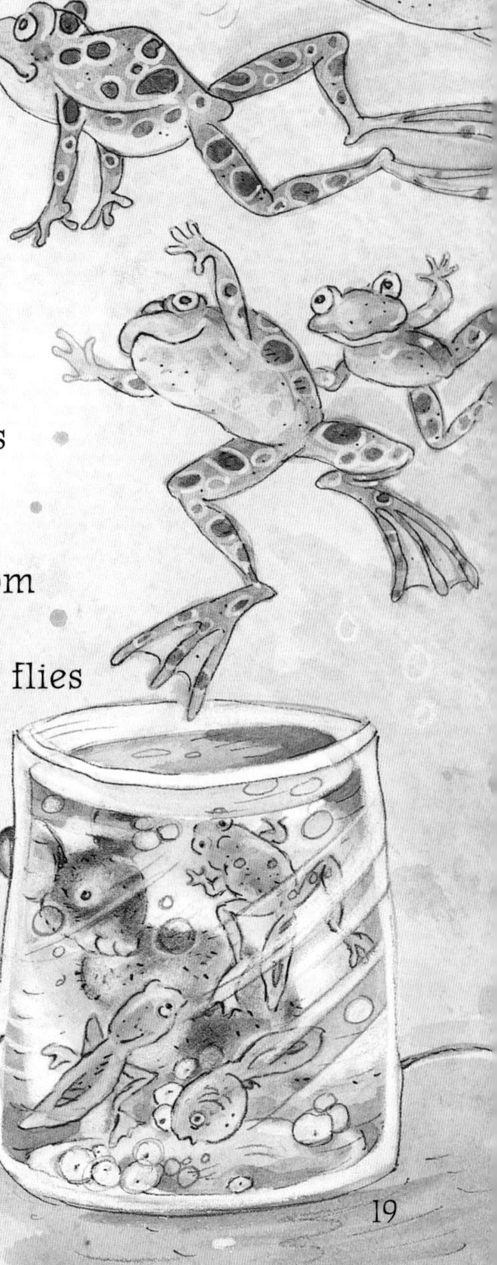

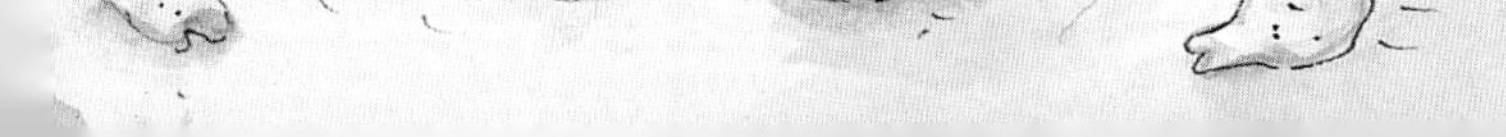

RAISE YOUR HAND IF YOU KNOW THE ANSWER

Poem for Two Voices

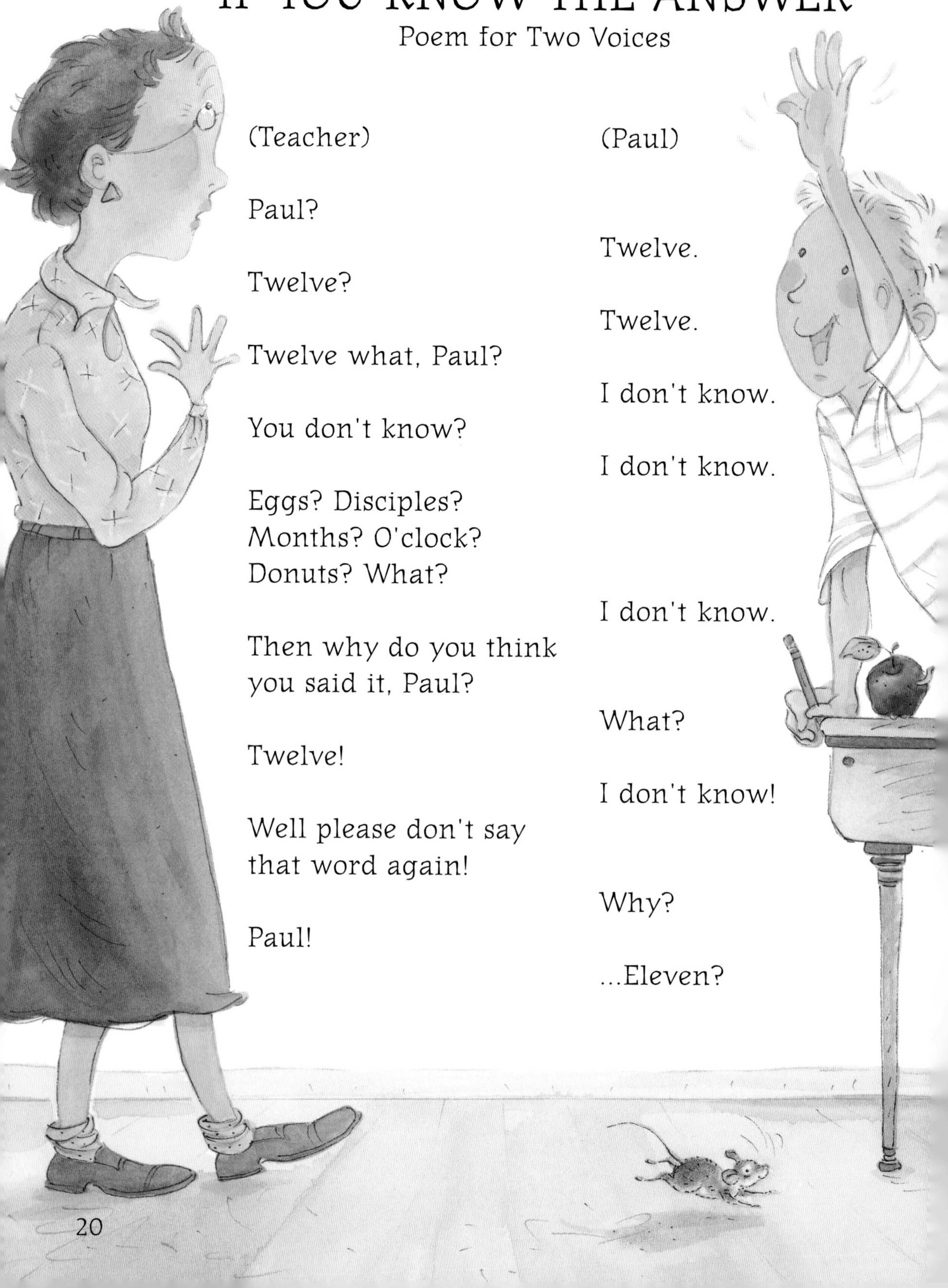

(Teacher)	(Paul)
Paul?	
	Twelve.
Twelve?	
	Twelve.
Twelve what, Paul?	
	I don't know.
You don't know?	
	I don't know.
Eggs? Disciples? Months? O'clock? Donuts? What?	
	I don't know.
Then why do you think you said it, Paul?	
	What?
Twelve!	
	I don't know!
Well please don't say that word again!	
	Why?
Paul!	
	...Eleven?

IN THE HALL

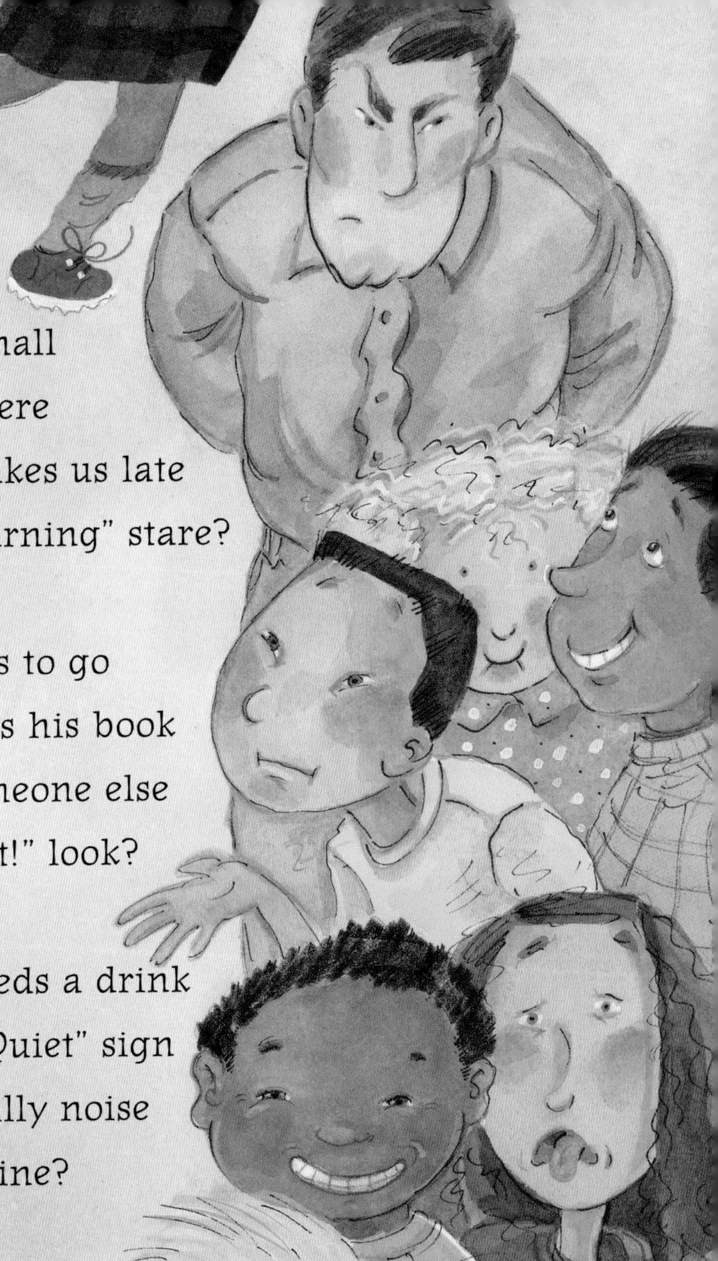

Don't you love it in the hall
Lining up to go somewhere
And someone always makes us late
And someone gets a "Warning" stare?

And someone always has to go
And someone else forgets his book
And someone tickles someone else
And gets us all a "Stop-it!" look?

And someone always needs a drink
And someone gets the "Quiet" sign
And someone makes a silly noise
At someone in another line?

Don't you love it best of all
Trying to line up in the hall?

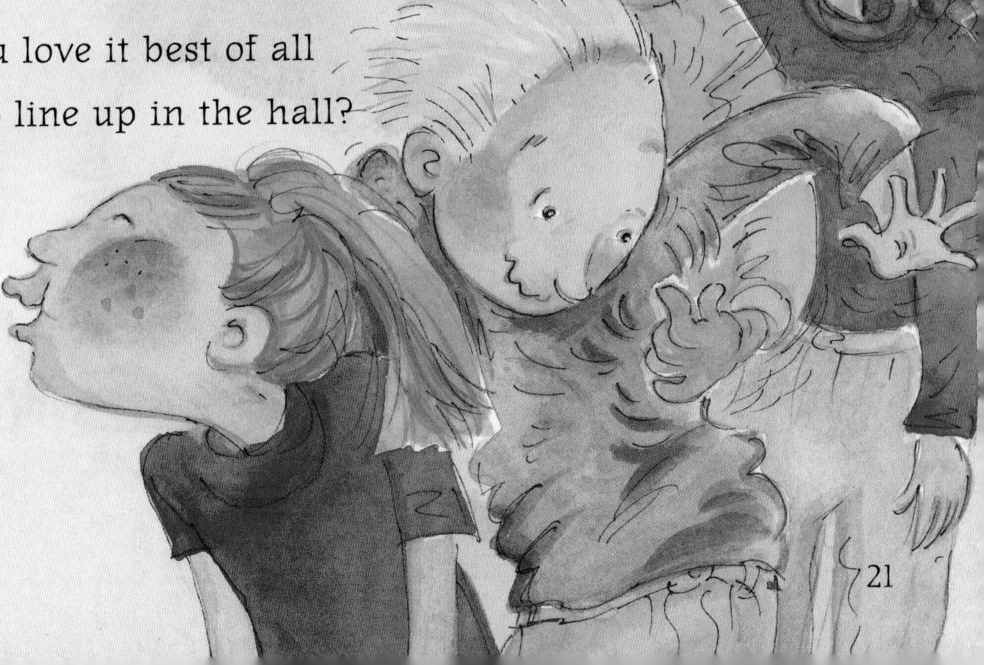

IT'S BETTER IF YOU DON'T KNOW

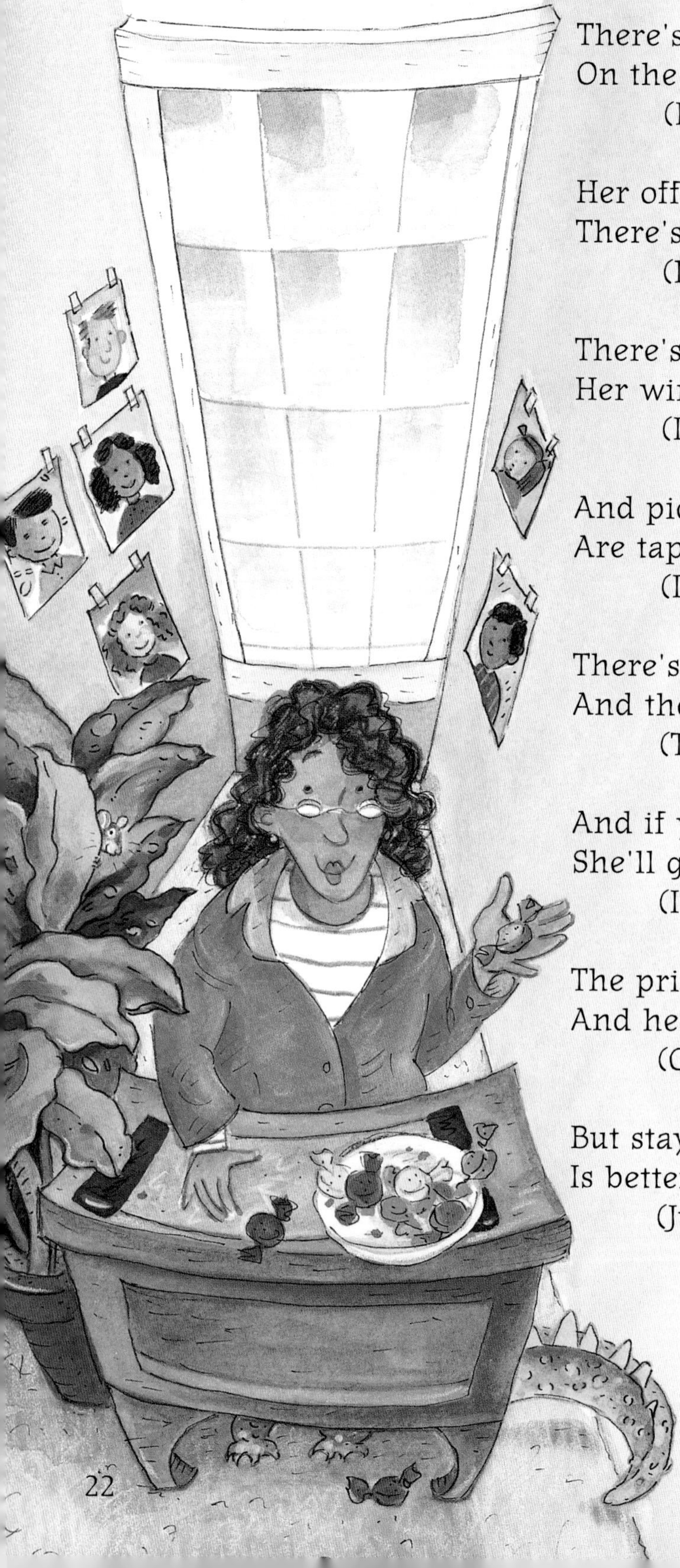

There's a Welcome sign
On the principal's door.
(But try not to go.)

Her office is long.
There's a rug on the floor.
(Never mind how I know.)

There's a plant by her desk.
Her windows are tall.
(I've heard kids say.)

And pictures of students
Are taped to the wall.
(It might be that way.)

There's a dish on her desk
And the candy is sweet.
(That's strictly a guess.)

And if you are lucky
She'll give you a treat.
(I don't know I confess.)

The principal is nice
And her candy is too.
(Or so I have heard.)

But staying in class
Is better for you.
(Just take my word!)

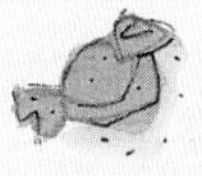

A MATTER OF OPINION

"Amos," said Teacher,
"You have to do better!
Can you offer me
Any suggestions?"

"Teacher," said Amos,
"The problem I think
Is my answers don't go
With your questions."

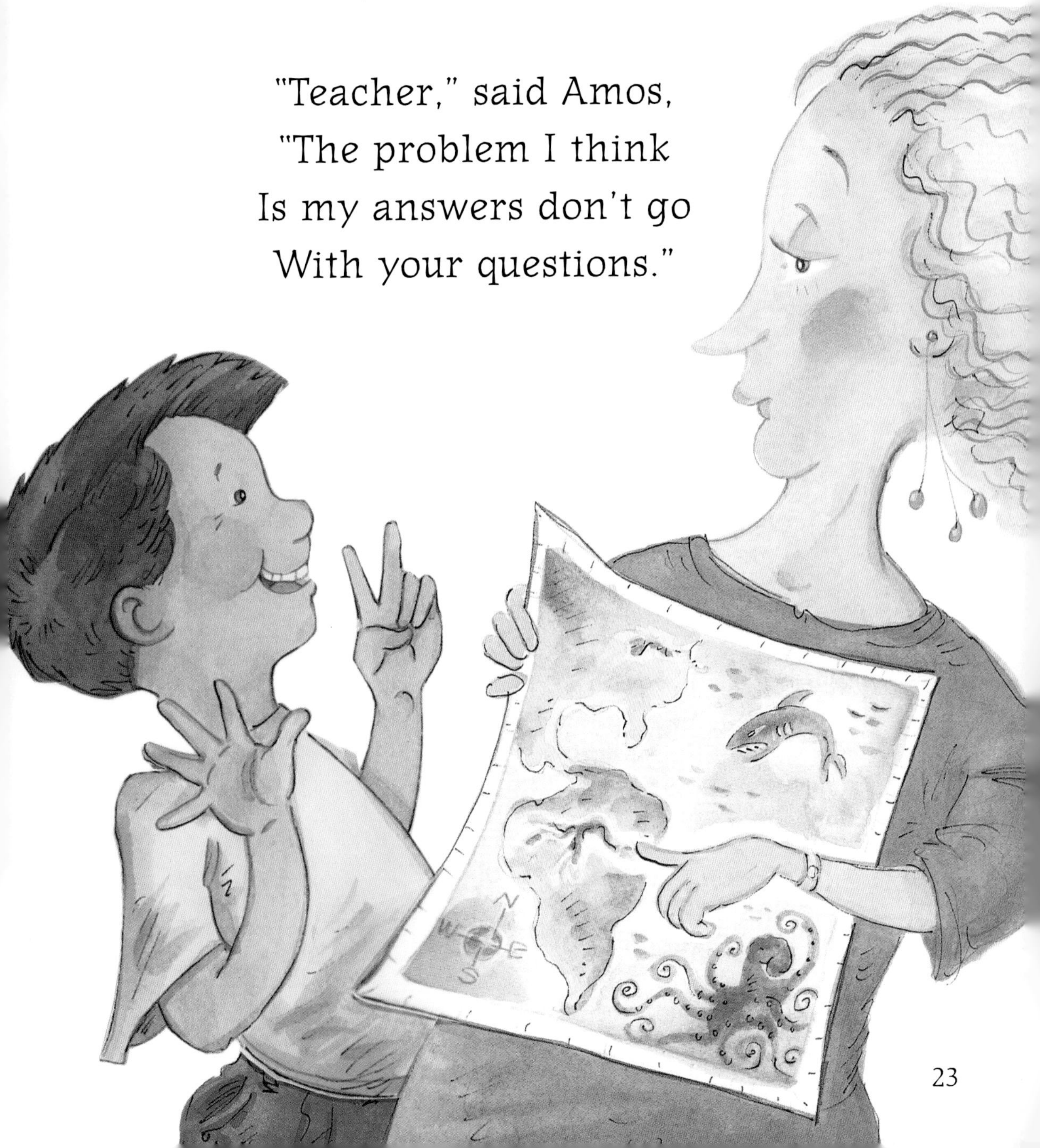
N
W
E
S

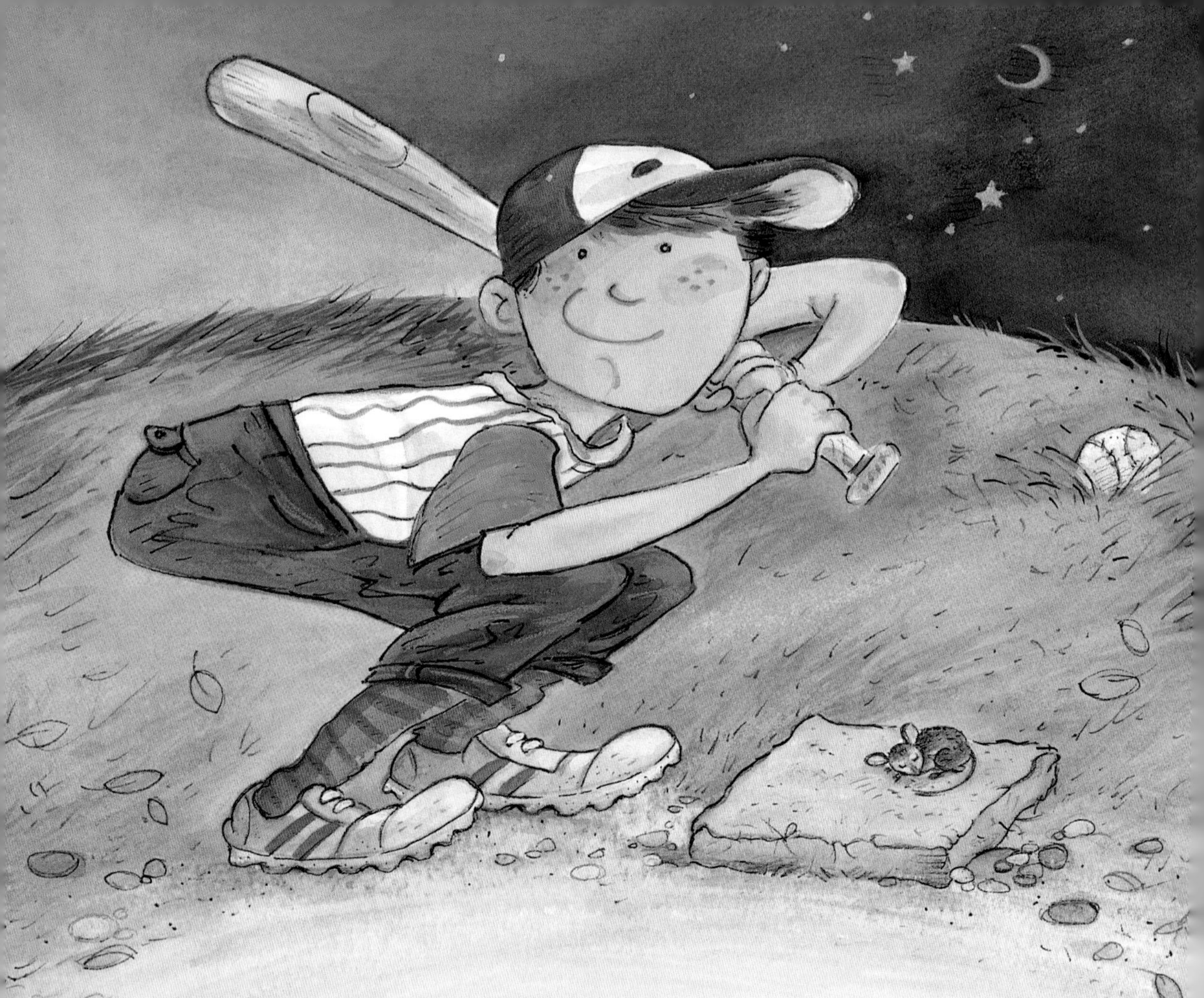

HOMERUN KING

I'm going to pound the cover off that ball!
I'm going to blast it clear outside the park!
I'm going to knock that ball so high
It won't come down again till after dark!

I'm going to break that ball in tiny pieces!
I'm going to smash it through the outfield wall!
I'm going to make the pitcher cry!
But first I'm going to have to hit the ball.

THE SECRET

I'll tell you a secret
That no one knows but me

Except for Lee
Who'd never rat—
We both know that—
So you can see
The secret's safe with Lee

So no one else will know
Except for us

Except for Russ
Who swore he'd eat
A moldy beet
If he discussed
The thing except with us

So it'll be Lee
And Russ and you and me
And Joe.

Joe won't swear
But we don't care!
Who can he tell
When all of us know?

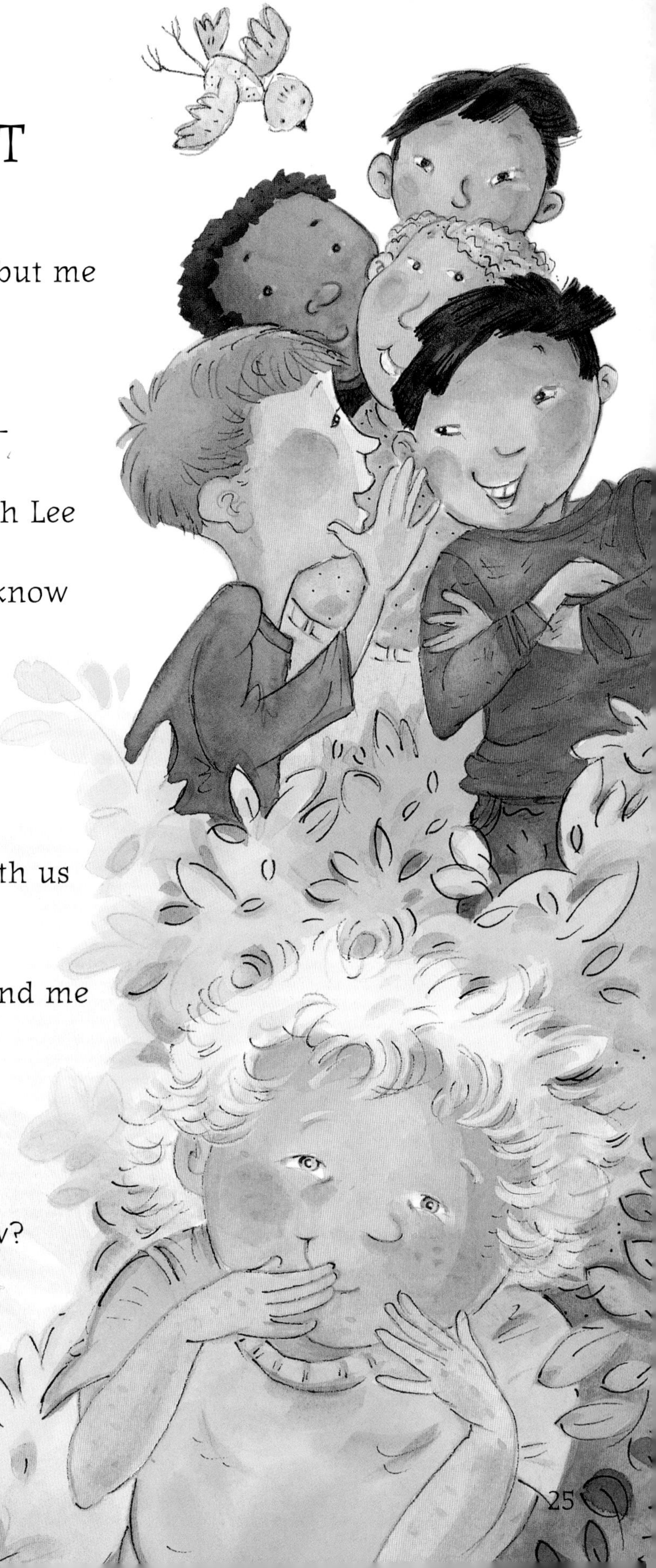

HAVE IT YOUR OWN WAY
Poem for Two Voices

(Isabelle)   (Teacher)

Me and Sally are pals!

                                Sally and I are pals.

I didn't know you knew her!

                                I don't.

Then why did you say,
"Me and Sally are pals?"

                                Sally and I are pals.

You said it again!
You said,
"Me and Sally are pals!"

                                Sally and I are pals!

Have it your own way.
You and her are pals,
But I don't believe it
And Sally won't neither!

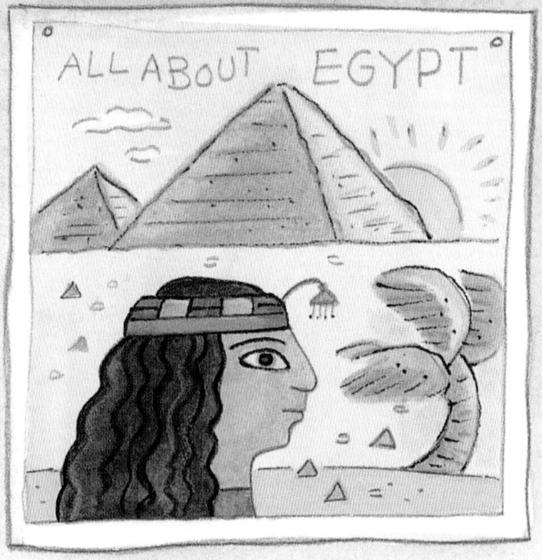
ALL ABOUT EGYPT

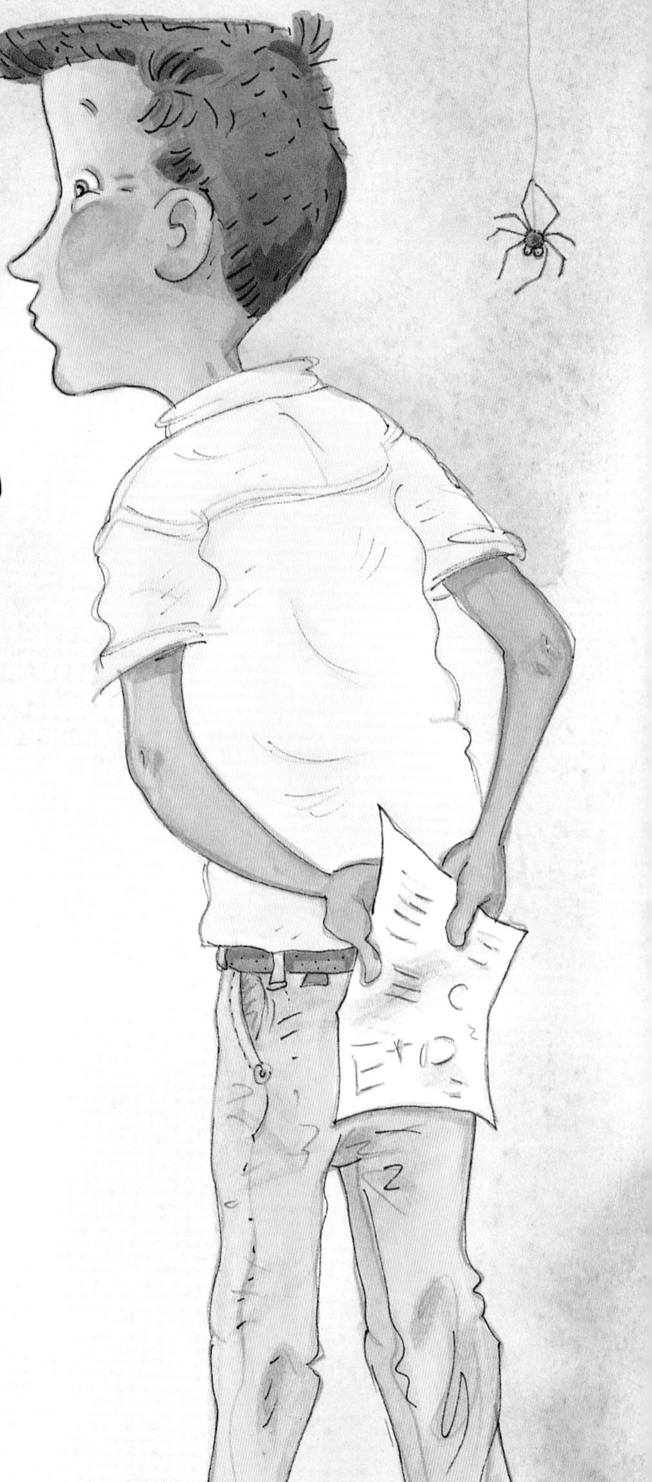

GRADE CARD

SPELLING
Can tell it.
Can't spell it.

MATH
Alath!
Can't subtrath!

HISTORY
History?
A mystery.

SCIENCE
Calls slugs
Bugs.

CONDUCT
Less saider
The better.

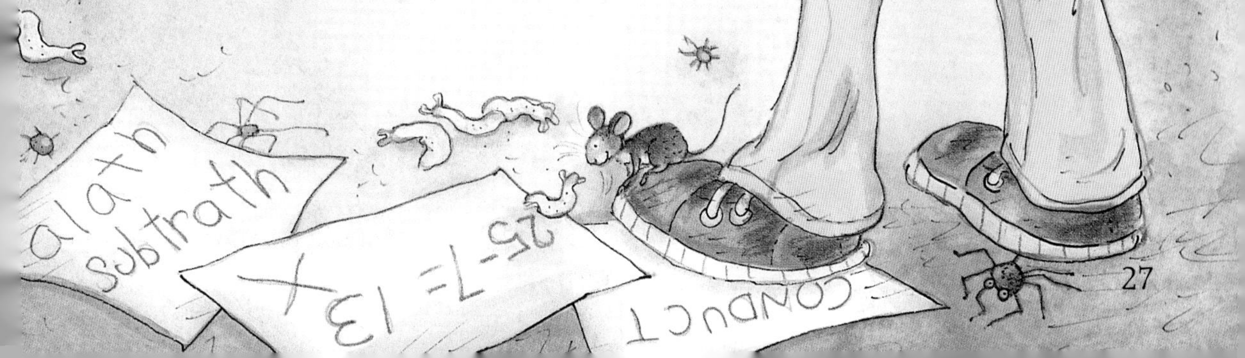
alath
subtrath
25-7=13
X
CONDUCT

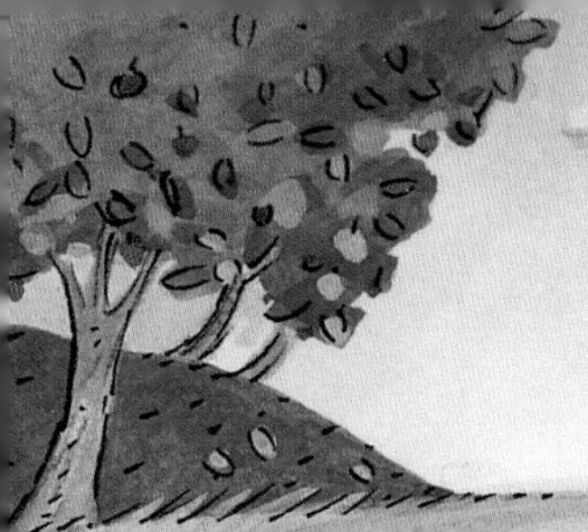

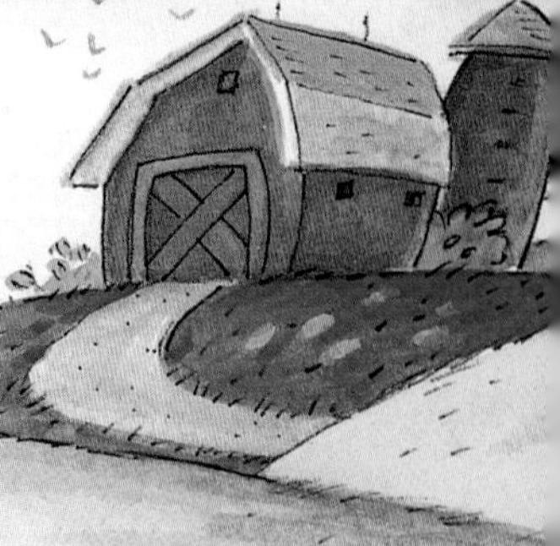

OUR FIELD TRIP

The minute we got off the bus
Paula had to sneeze.
A big old bee stung Irving's arm
And Tony began to wheeze.

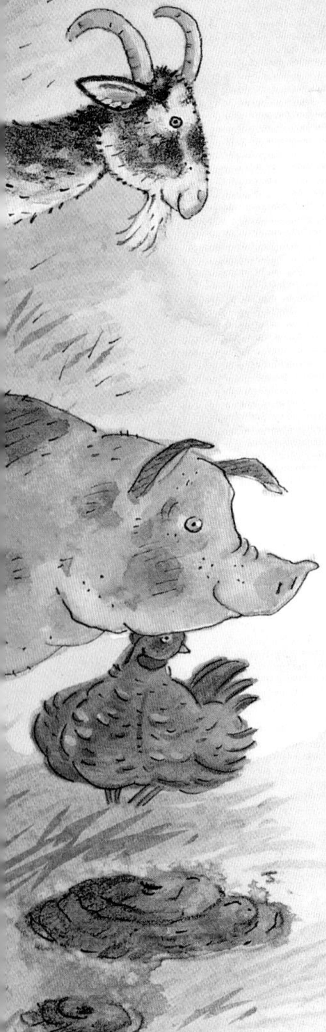

Ruby tried to pet a pig
And lost a tennis shoe.
Paula sneezed her glasses off
And lost them in the goo.

Tony wheezed and rubbed his eyes
And Irving slapped at bees
And Ruby fussed about her shoe
Till Paula had to sneeze.

She blew her whole retainer out
And bounced it off a hen.
She made a face and wiped it off
And put it in again.

Then Ruby lost her other shoe
Fooling with the pig
And Tony wheezed and rubbed his eyes
And Irving's arm got big.

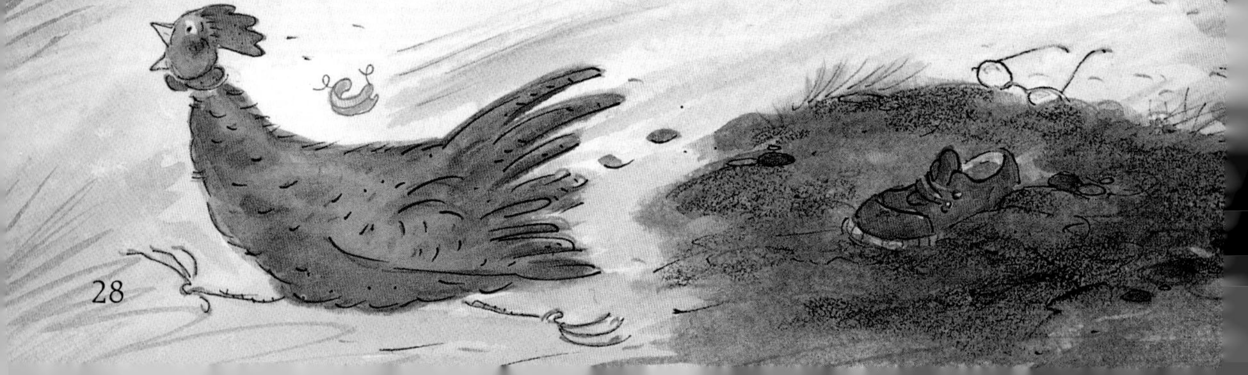

Paula stepped in you-know-what
And tracked it on the bus
And Ruby cried about her shoes
And caused an awful fuss.

Except for wheezes, glasses, shoes,
And the bee on Irving's arm,
Of all the trips we've ever had
We really loved the farm!

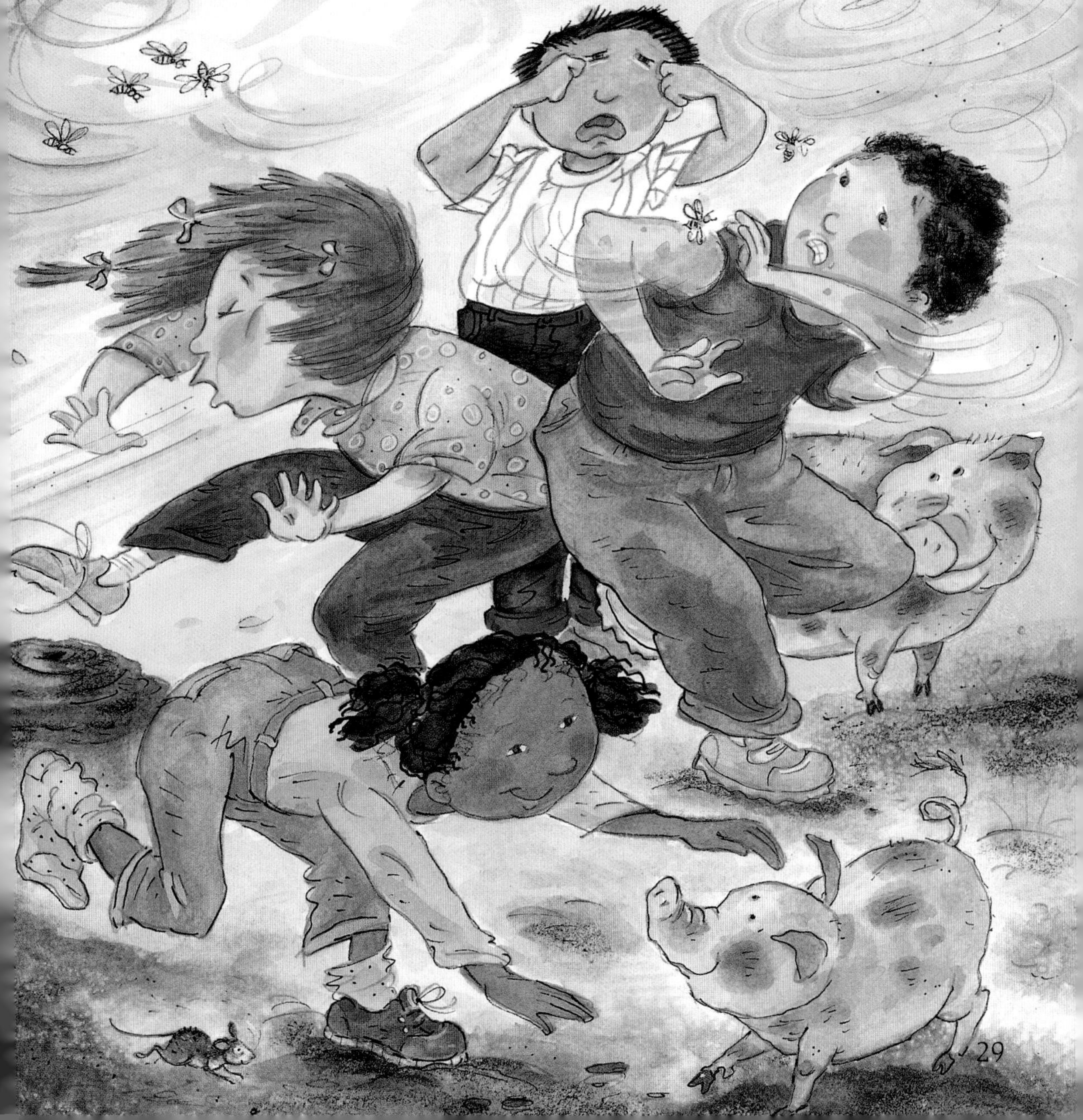

TEACHER'S EYES

Our teacher has eyes
in the back of her head.

She looks at the board
but sees me instead.

She calls my name,
My face turns red.

Our teacher has eyes
in the back of her head!

WE'LL BE BACK!

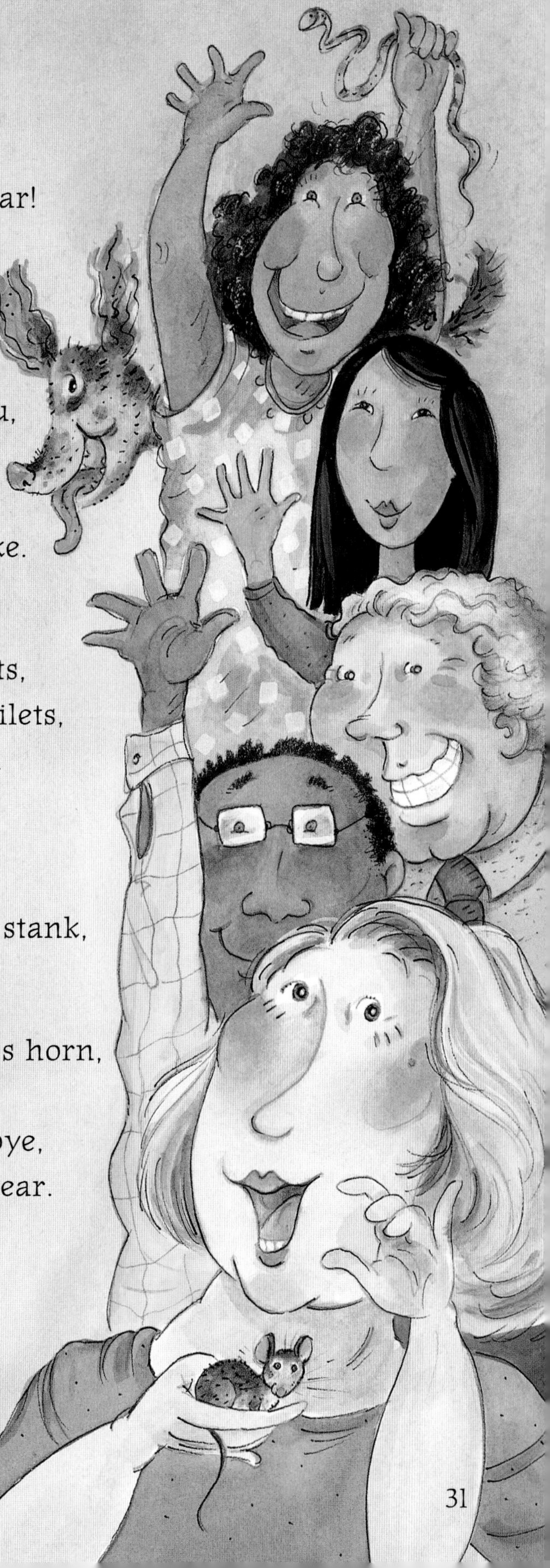

We really learned a lot this year!
Opal Johnson broke her arm,
Martin's dog got into school,
Carlos tripped a fire alarm.

Grace gave half the class the flu,
Ruby lost her garter snake,
Cecie fell and chipped a tooth,
Nate threw up his birthday cake.

Carolina got a splinter,
Tyler Williams ripped his pants,
Someone stopped up all the toilets,
Kris knocked over all our ants.

Sasha had her tonsils out,
Ivan ate his contact lens,
Our worm collection died and stank,
Mrs. Purrington had twins.

We found the snake in Ashley's horn,
Bruno Benson pierced his ear,
All our teachers waved good-bye,
But we'll be back again next year.

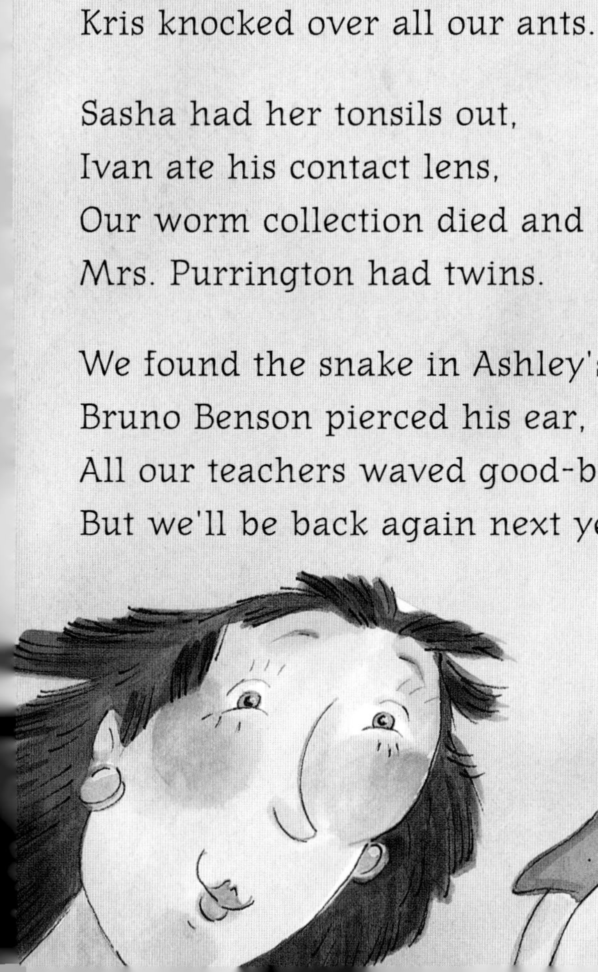

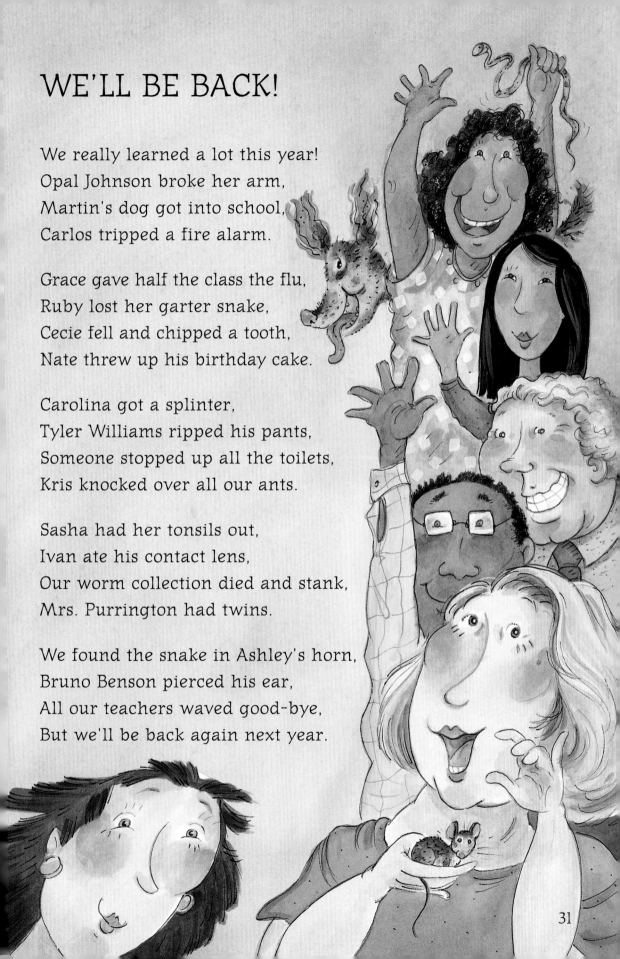

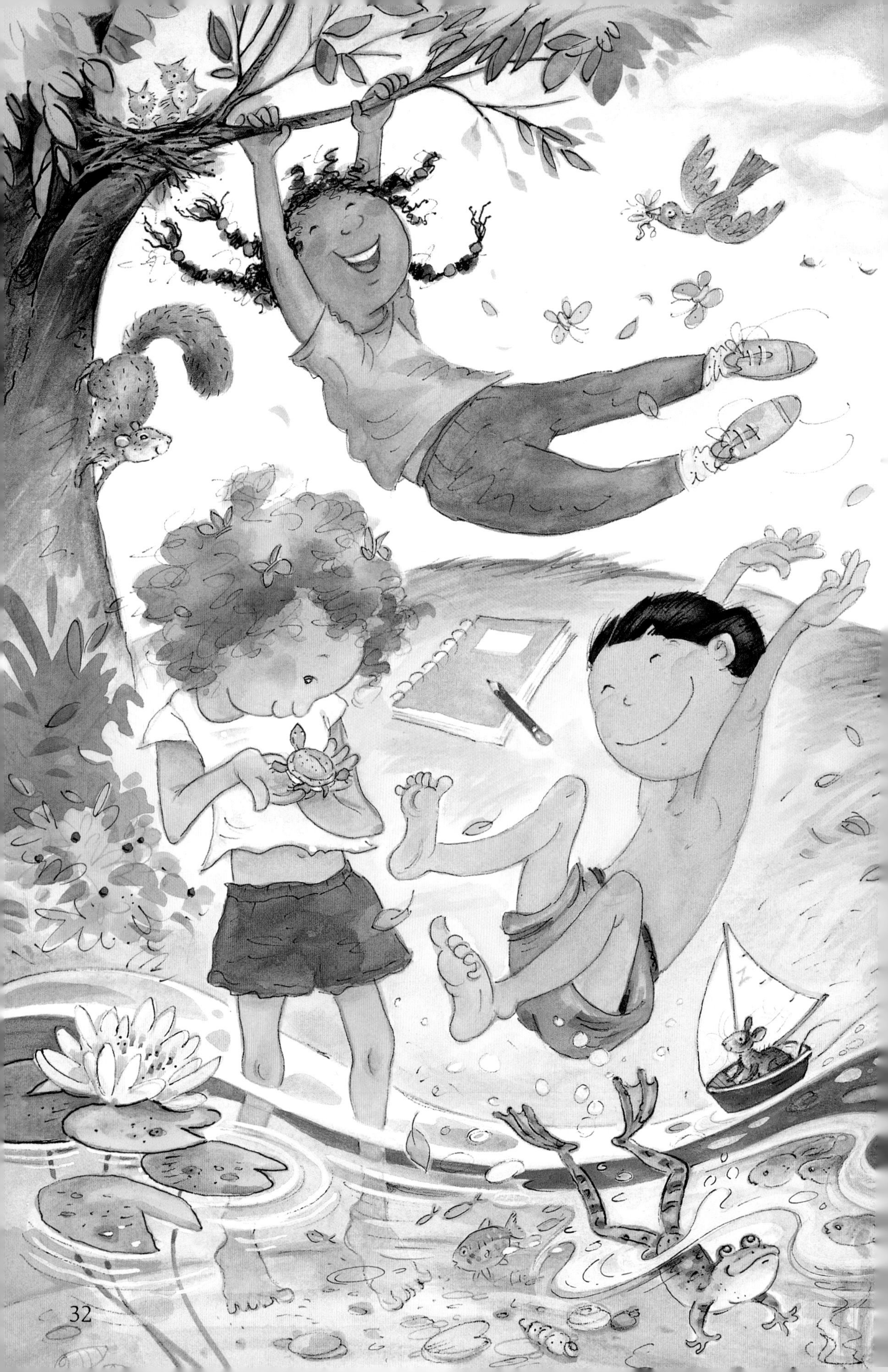